The Winter Tree

ISBN: 978-1-70210-107-3

The Winter Tree

by

Stuart James

"Hold on!"

Chapter One

It was a Sunday morning at the time of year when autumn blurred into winter. Lorrie woke up. She pulled on her yellow, spotty dressing gown and jumped into her pink, fluffy slippers. She skipped over to the window and looked out.

Just beyond the garden, over the brook and on top of the little hill there stood a little tree. The tree was partly smudged out by fog. It looked sad. The night had been windy and only a few leaves now hung on its branches. Looking just like teardrops.

"Poor tree," thought Lorrie. So she breathed on the window pane and, with her finger, she drew a smiling face. In a moment the circle of breath was gone. But the tree still looked sad.

Quickly, Lorrie ate her porridge. She wrapped herself in her big thick coat, the one with the furry hood and the big buttons, and she pulled on her wellies.

At the top of the garden she opened the gate, skipped across the brook and after several puffs up the little hill she stood in front of the tree. "Hello, tree," she said.

"My name is Lorrie. I don't expect you to tell me your name. Or even to talk. Trees don't do that do they? But I thought you looked cold and sad. And I would like to make you happy again."

Over the last few weeks, Lorrie had watched the leaves turn from green to yellow to gold to red... and to brown. But now there were barely any left. And this made the tree look very sad indeed.

Lorrie ran back indoors to find daddy.

She found him, sitting in his favourite chair, just a spit and a crackle from the fire. He peeped above the morning newspaper.

"Daddy, could we bring the little tree on the hill into the house? So it would be nice and warm in the winter."

"Don't be silly, Lorrie," said daddy. "A tree belongs outside. That's where it is meant to be." He disappeared again behind the newspaper.

"Oh," thought Lorrie. "But it's lost all its leaves and looks… very cold." She imagined how she would feel if she was a tree and she had lost all of her leaves. "Brrrr!"

Daddy looked up from his paper again but Lorrie was gone.

In fact, she'd had an idea. She emerged from the garden shed pushing a squeaky old wheelbarrow. She wheeled it half way up the hill and began to busily collect leaves from the ground.

A robin fluttered down onto one of the branches of the tree. He cocked his head one way, then the other, curiously watching what she was doing.

When there was a small pile of leaves in the wheelbarrow, Lorrie stood back and clapped her hands together. "Now to put them back on the tree... Hmmmm. But how?" she wondered.

Ten minutes later...

"Oh dear. This isn't going to work." Lorrie had begun to stick the leaves back on the tree with some sticky tape. But the branches were wet and the leaves just wouldn't stick very well. Then a stray blast of wind blew most of them off again.

"Even if these leaves did stick, I'm not sure you would be very happy with the way you looked anyway." The leaves were mostly soggy and brown.

Chapter One

Disheartened, Lorrie wheeled the wheelbarrow back down the hill, back over the brook, back through the gate and back into the shed at the bottom of the garden. The wheelbarrow squeaked all the way. Lorrie sighed. She would have to think of something else.

Later, when the moon came out and the sun was nearly gone, the wind blew again.

It was the kind of wind which would turn a brolly inside out and your coat too if left unbuttoned.

It rattled the letterbox and whistled in the chimney breast. Somehow it crept into the house and Lorrie felt its breath upon her ankles. It seemed there was a storm coming. Lorrie looked out of the window and gazed up at the brightest star in the sky. She made a wish. She wished that the little tree would be alright.

Tucked up in bed, Lorrie held her little toy bunny close and she fell asleep. But it wasn't long before she was disturbed by a noise.

The curtains flapped and the windows shuddered as the wind sprayed rain and blew snow into her bedroom. She pulled on her dressing gown, grabbed bunny, hurried down the stairs and ran outside into the darkness.

The wind tried to turn her around. It seemed to be telling her to go back to the house. She was sure she heard it hiss, "This is no place for a little girl!" But she fumbled her way through the gate. She stumbled over the brook — her bare foot slipping on a stone and plunging into the icy cold water. But still she carried on.

She ran as fast as she could to the top of the hill where she threw her arms around the tree and tried with all her might to save it from the grip of the wind. Bunny too was trying to help. He was clinging to a branch, his little legs kicking as he was tossed to and fro.

There was a creak.
Then a loud crack.
"Hold on, bunny!"

Lorrie tumbled forwards. The tree had been uprooted. In one last show of strength, the wind hurled the tree and bunny high into the air. Tree and bunny cartwheeled like acrobats, higher and higher and higher into the sky until they were only specks against the shape of the moon. "Bunny! Tree!" Lorrie cried.

She caught her breath and ran back to the house. She slipped and slid down the hill, splashed through the brook, fell through the gate and threw herself at the kitchen door. It was now locked. She hammered with both her fists as loud as she could.

"Mummy! Daddy! Let me in!"

Mummy and daddy quickly appeared at the door. They found her sitting up in bed, sobbing.

"What is the matter, Lorrie? Have you had a bad dream?"

"Dream?... No," said Lorrie.

"It's Bunny!... The tree... They're gone."

Chapter One

But Bunny was not gone. He lay still and quietly on her pillow, just as fluffy, and unaware of the night's adventure.

Daddy picked up Bunny and put him into Lorrie's arms.

"Bunny?" she whispered.

She looked around. The curtains were drawn, the windows shut. She ran across the room and peered out into the night. As she made out the vague shape of the tree, her heart leapt with joy. The tree was standing on top of the hill in exactly the same place it had stood before she had gone to bed.

There was no mud on her dressing gown, which was folded neatly over a chair, just as she'd left it. Her feet were dry and the wind outside was a gentle one.

"Oh," said Lorrie. "Yes, I think I've had a bad dream."

"Just your colour!"

Chapter Two

The next morning, autumn seemed to have gone and winter had painted the whole scene white with frost.

Lorrie had risen early with one of her best ideas and she was busy exploring the bottoms of drawers and the backs of wardrobes.

"Lovely!... Perfect!... Hmm. Not warm enough... Ah! This will do."

Soon her arms were wrapped around a big basket full of scarves, mittens, jumpers, hats and socks.

The grass, sparkling with frost, crunched softly under her feet as she walked to the top of the garden. She opened the gate, carefully crossed the brook and trudged up the little hill.

"Morning, tree," she said, putting the basket down on the ground. "Cold isn't it!" Picking out a pink, spotty woollen scarf, she held it up in front of the tree.

"Just your colour!"

She tied it around one of the topmost branches. Then she picked something else from the basket. A blue mitten. She placed it on the end of another branch. Then a scarf again, this time green, its braid catching the sunlight with a hundred colours or more… And so on. Until the basket was empty and the tree was dressed for winter.

"There. That should keep you warm," said Lorrie and she felt a warm glow herself.

The tree was a rainbow of colour.

Greens and golds and reds and yellows and pinks and blues and blends and twists of all those colours made a wonderful sight.

"Bye then, tree!" said Lorrie. "Now I have to go to school."
She picked up the basket, hurried down the little hill, skipped
over the brook, through the gate and back to the house.

"Bye, mummy," she said as she set off to school.

"Bye, daddy!" she shouted. Daddy didn't hear. He was upstairs,
busily looking for a scarf to wear for work. Where could it be?

Lorrie was very happy with herself and if it hadn't been so
frosty, she would probably have skipped all the way to school.
She walked with her friend, Helen, who lived in a house just over
the road. Lorrie told her all about the tree and Helen couldn't
wait to see it.

The morning passed quickly. The afternoon came and so too
did the snow. Big chunky snowflakes fell like balls of cotton
wool from the pearl white sky. All the children gazed out of the
classroom window, looking with wonder as it turned whiter
and whiter outside.

Lorrie's mind wondered all the way home, out into the garden, over the brook and up the little hill.

It snowed. And snowed.

At last the bell rang for home time. Lorrie and Helen made their way home as quickly as they could, slipping every now and again on the snowy path, but giggling all the way. Hundreds and hundreds of snowflakes swirled in the light of the street lamps.

Soon after saying 'goodbye' to Helen, Lorrie was back home. Her rosy cheeks glistened where snowflakes had melted. "Hello, darling," said mummy, taking her coat. "Have you had a good day?" Lorrie nodded.

The house was warm. The fire blazed in the lounge, and in the kitchen, an apple and blackberry pie — Mmmmm — Lorrie's favourite, baked in the oven.

Lorrie thought about the tree. Even if daddy was right, and the place for a tree was outside, she hoped that the cold, wintery night wouldn't feel quite as cold anymore.

It snowed all night and most of the following day. School closed early, so Lorrie and Helen went to see the tree together. Although, by now, the tree was mostly covered with snow, Helen said how pretty it looked.

* * *

That winter was one of the coldest for a long time. The cold brought more snow and that, in turn, brought sledging to the hills.

The excited, mingling breaths of the children hung in the air like a happy fog. They sledged. They snowballed. They laughed and squealed and hoorayed and sang until the fading light would bring them back indoors.

Soon all of Lorrie's friends knew about the tree and they grew
fond of it too, sometimes bringing the odd item of clothing which
they no longer needed.

Christmas came and even the Christmas Eve church service
took an unusual twist. It ended with a procession down the lane
and up the little hill to where carols were sung around Lorrie's
tree. The bright yellow flames of the lanterns danced in the night,
hinting at the colours of the fabrics hung on the tree's branches.
Everyone from the village seemed to be there, and every face
was lit with joy.

Eventually, as is commonplace at around the same time each year, the winter began to melt away.

It was another bedtime and Lorrie looked out of her bedroom window. The tree looked enchanting, glowing gently in the light of a full moon.

Lorrie thought the tree looked happier too. Perhaps it was a trick of the light. Daddy had spoken of such a thing before when Lorrie could see things that he could not. But Lorrie felt, in her heart, that at least the tree wasn't so sad anymore.

She slept soundly that night, and dreamed dreams inspired by the adventures of those wonderful last few months.

Chapter Two

Then late one afternoon came the fog...

Chapter Three

The next morning, the crocuses were the first up, bravely poking their curious heads above the soil.

With the winter receding over the high ground and the late frosts dwindling, the crocuses were soon followed by tulips and daffodils. And then buds appeared on the roses and the trees.

Lorrie decided it was perhaps time to undress the tree for spring. So she gathered up all the scarves, mittens, jumpers, hats and socks into the basket. Well, almost 'all'. She was sure the tree had already grown because she couldn't quite reach the pink, spotty woollen scarf tied to the highest branch.

"Oh, well," she said. "It does look rather good on you."

The Winter Tree

 As is nature's way, spring blossomed... and summer bloomed. And the little tree on top of the little hill, didn't seem quite so little anymore. The leaves were greener and more plentiful too as the tree's limbs stretched further skyward.

 Summer ambled by in its casual, carefree way. Lorrie played games, read books and lay down in the shade of the tree to watch, through flickering leaves, the clouds drifting idly overhead.

 Eventually the days became shorter and the shadows longer. A robin appeared again in the tree. Finding the topmost branch a little high, he dropped to a branch a little closer to the ground.

 The robin, the blackberries bursting in the hedgerows and the softly blushing foliage of the trees hinted that autumn was just around the corner. Occasionally, a chill wind, off course from the north, was reminder that winter would soon come again.

Then late one afternoon came the fog. Lorrie was looking for the best pine cones. She looked back at her house and could see the warm light from the kitchen. The light was fuzzy but she could see it. Already it was getting darker so she knew it was time to be indoors.

But "just one more pine cone," she thought.

Her eyes searched amongst the leaves and the twigs strewn around her feet. "Ah, there's one!" She picked it up and put it in her pocket with the others. The fog had become thicker. She looked up. Where was the light? It was gone. Where was the tree? She could just make out a vague shape. Was that it? But in a moment it was gone again. And the fog crept mysteriously around her.

Lorrie called out. "Mummy! Daddy!" They would be expecting her in by now. But there was no reply. All she could hear was the occasional twittering of birds in the trees, safely settled and unwilling to take flight into the murky dusk. Then a car whooshed by in the distance. She was lost. Lorrie had kept walking and she was sure by now that she was going the wrong way. It felt colder too. She was very frightened.

Then she felt something tap her shoulder. There was a breeze and something brushed against her nose. It was a little golden leaf. A familiar looking leaf. It fluttered gently in front of her face. Just like a butterfly. Then it pirouetted behind her. She turned around and there it was again, neither rising nor falling but dancing in the air right in front of her.

She reached out her hand. But the leaf spun away and this time brushed against her ear. She was sure she heard a gentle whisper. "Follow me."

"Follow me"

So she did.

Occasionally, in the drifting fog, Lorrie would lose sight of the leaf. But then its golden colour would burn brighter so she'd see it again and catch up.

It wasn't long before she heard a familiar voice calling her name... and getting closer.

"Coming, mummy!" she shouted.

Soon she could see a light again, spilling from the kitchen window and a crack in the door. And then she saw mummy. The leaf spun into the air and then gently fell to the ground, coming to rest at the foot of the tree.

"Thank you," said Lorrie, and she hurried down the hill, over the brook, through the gate and into the welcoming arms of mummy.

"Is tea ready, yet?" she wondered.

A few weeks passed by. The last of the leaves had fallen from the tree and as the first sparkling frosts cast their magical spell, Lorrie made that short journey again.

And just as she had done a year ago, she stood before the tree and set down a basket full of scarves, mittens, jumpers, hats and socks.

But this time, on a piece of string tied around a branch of the tree, there was an envelope. It was addressed 'To Lorrie.'

She untied the envelope, opened it and read the note inside.

To Lorrie

"Thank you for looking after me last winter.
But you've no need to worry this year. I'll be fine
without scarves, mittens, jumpers, hats and socks.
No matter how cold it shall get, how hard the
winds shall blow or how much the snow shall fall,
my heart will be kept warm by the thought
of the kindness of a very special friend."

Lorrie smiled, tucked the note back into
the envelope and put it into her pocket.

The Winter Tree

Another winter passed. The tree appeared none the worse for the wind, the frost or the snow.

When spring arrived again, the tree dressed itself in a beautiful white blossom. This didn't last long and soon fell like a gentle snow. New leaves unfurled to absorb the warm, gentle rays of sunlight which lasted longer with each day.

And so on. The seasons came and went and came back again. Lorrie made daisy-chains. She built the biggest snowman you'd ever seen. She read books. She played hide and seek with friends. She licked ice lollies, picked blackberries. She skipped, sledged and kicked leaves. In winter coats, or summer frills, there was always fun to be had. Lorrie and her friends danced around the tree, singing, laughing and having the very best of times.

As the seasons gently rolled into years,
the tree grew... and grew... and grew.
And meanwhile, as little girls will do,
Lorrie grew up too.

It was a Sunday morning at the time of year when autumn blurred into winter. It was a day in which all colour was gone.

But if you were to look up at the tree, high amongst the branches, you might see a pink, spotty woollen scarf flapping gently in the breeze. Clinging on, but only just. Like the last leaf of autumn.

Then there was a gust of wind, a swirl of leaves and at last, finally unravelling from around the branch to which it had been tied a long while ago, down zig-zagged the pink, spotty woollen scarf. A little frayed, a little weathered, a little less pink than it had once been, the scarf landed softly on the ground.

A little girl, with big blue eyes and pink rose petal cheeks, happened to be pushing her dolly in a little pushchair up the hill.

Chapter Three

The wind hushed the rustling of the remaining leaves on the tree. The morning seemed to sigh and a little robin landed upon one of the tree's branches. He tilted his head to one side, then back again and he flew away.

The girl looked up at the sky. It looked like it might snow.

Wrapping the scarf around dolly's neck, the little girl pushed the pushchair back down the hill, over the brook and through a squeaky old gate.

"Let's go and show mummy what we've found," she said.

The End

Printed in Great Britain
by Amazon

36397367R00023